Essays from Dysfunctional Families

Dean K. Brent

Essays from Dysfunctional Families©

Dean K. Brent

Library of Congress

Published by: Nodnol Publishing

Editor: Michael Valentine

Cover Design by LGD

Printed in London, England

CONTENTS

Michael R.

Goshen, Indiana

I was born and raised in a town in Indiana named Goshen, along with one brother and one sister, both younger than me. We grew up in a home that was very confusing, and as a child I never understood why my parents did what they did. They knew how to put on an act that could rival Hollywood, even though they were never professional actors. My father was a construction worker and made pretty good dough. We were never needy. When he came home though he was exhausted and rarely spent much time with us. Every now and then he would take us to the park and sometimes to exciting places such as zoos, museums, sporting games, and sometimes the theatre.

My mother on the other hand worked part time as a seamstress. She was home more often and she would take us out more than our father. The only thing that had me, that had all of us confused was their constant change in character. After living with them for some time you just got used to the routine. On Friday and Saturday nights we were left home alone. At first I wasn't sure where my parents were going, but as soon as I reached an age where I could understand, it was clear. I wasn't exactly sure, but I knew it was a bar or club of some sort. They came home drunk and sometimes high.

During their "under the influence" times they would do and say things that I am sure they were unaware they were doing. One Friday night my father came home and asked me to turn the water on in the tub and make sure it was hot. He said he wanted to take a hot bath. I asked him if he was sure and he said don't ask me questions just do what I say. So I went into the bathroom and I turned the water on and made sure it was hot. After a few minutes he got naked in front of me and got in the tub. All I heard was a scream that was louder than any I had ever heard before. He jumped out of the tub and ran in my direction like the Roadrunner in the cartoons. I shook with fear at that moment. Not sure what to do I just stood there. My father spat out every curse word he could think of and threw the words at me along with whipping me like a runaway slave .

That was the first time I ever really got beat, but not the last. All I can remember is the pain and the words, "That was too mother fucking hot, you bitch." The words and the hits were like hearing a cow meow, just too bizzare for me. My mother laid unconscious on the couch the whole time, while my siblings cowered in their room.

Another crazy event I can remember was a Saturday night my mother returned home before my father and she was pretty high. Before leaving she had asked my sister to wash the dishes. Because we knew how crazy our parents were we always obeyed their every word. We made sure we completed all chores and when one had problems the other two would help to keep the peace in the house. When my mother returned there were no dishes in the sink, they had all been washed, dried and put away. But for whatever reason she saw dishes in the sink. She woke my sister up, dragged her to the sink and screamed, "What the fuck is this?"

My sister was scared, my brother and I watched making sure my mother didn't see us. My sister responded fearfully and timidly asked, "What's wrong?"

My mother replied with, "Didn't I ask you to wash the dishes?"

My sister responded, "Yes, Mother, and I did."

"Then why are there dishes in the sink?"

"Mother, there are none," my sister said, trying in vain to reason with her. "Are you okay?"

At that point my mother got angry and cursed my sister out as if she was a woman sleeping with her husband. My mother began to shake her and that's when I stepped in and tried to pull my sister away. My mother dropped her and grabbed me and began to slap me. I tried in vain to show her that there were no dishes in the sink, but she just could not see. That was the first and last time my mother beat me.

My parents did many things to us all on many occasions that are just shameful and in some cases too unreal to believe, but I swear to them all. We mostly received verbal abuse and occasionally physical abuse from our father. Our mother would only abuse us with her words, but she was too drunk to remember anything she said. What confused me the most was they would be sober enough to take us to church every Sunday afternoon at St. John's Catholic Church. Their presence at church was completely different than their presence on Friday and Saturday nights. It was even different than their regular weekday routine. I could not understand for the life of me how they could be three different people in just one week, every week. That's why I always thought they were the best actors. I am pretty sure no one at the bars they frequented ever saw their Catholic Church face and the church never saw their bar/club face.

Today my parents live alone and they are too old to go bar hopping. I believe they have quit the drugs and alcohol, but they still go to church. Sometimes my siblings and I sit and wonder if maybe we dreamed it all, because our parents never apologized and when we get together I really don't know if they have any memory of the abuse they put us through. They talk as if nothing bad ever happened and as if we all lived a regular family life, which of course we never did. There are days where I feel like talking to them about it, but I always fear the worst so I just sit on these memories trying to ignore them. Still, no matter how many days go by without me thinking about them, they always return. As silly as it sounds, to this day I do not take baths and do not know when I will be okay to do so.

My brother has a son and my sister has two children, one of each. However, I am not married nor have children and it is simply because I am afraid I will become my parents, which is something I never want to be. There are days I wish my life could have been different, but then again without the craziness I had as I child I wouldn't have the job I have now. I am a counselor; I counsel families and children who are in abusive situations. In every case my goal is to end the abuse or send the children to a home where they can experience love. Sometimes I get jealous because I am helping children receive what they deserve from their parents, love, which is something I never received from mine.

Tara W.

Riverton, Wyoming

Riverton is a city in Fremont County, Wyoming. It is the largest city in the county and a city I have not visited for over ten years nor do I plan to. The city itself is nice, but it holds too many bad memories. Just about every store, library, school, or house I go by reminds me of my past that I hate to admit is mine. I was born in Lander and at the age of five we moved to Riverton. I was the only child of a single mother. My mother did her best in raising me, but as we all know raising a child was never meant for one person to do. I only saw my father on Christmas and my birthday. He moved to Lusk, which is not close so traveling back and forth was not something either one of us did regularly.

My mother worked three jobs to keep a roof over our head, food on our table, and clothes on our back. She worked as a secretary at a doctor's office during the day, she worked part-time at night at the local supermarket and on Saturdays she worked as a bartender. So as you can imagine I spent most of my life alone. Sundays were the only days we spent together. I loved Sundays. We would wake up in the morning and she would make the best breakfast. Every Sunday was different. The menu would include: cereal, hot cereal, home-made waffles, pancakes, toast, eggs, potatoes, grits, turkey sausages, turkey bacon, fresh fruit, bagels, French toast, fruit cereal, and sometimes fresh fish. She would always make different combinations and being with her was such a blessing. We would go to church and afterwards she would take me out to the park, or to a movie, or sometimes we would just talk. It was the only day that I spent all day with her. Saturdays we would spend the mornings together. We spent most Saturdays shopping before she would have to leave for work.

On weekdays I would see her in the morning and late afternoons, but she would be resting most of the time. I was told to stay in the house or nearby while she was away at work, but it was pretty difficult to do so. There is only so much you can do in a house before you go stir crazy. I spent most of my time with my friends. They loved hanging out with me only because I was the only one who lived in a house where parents were not around. They would come over and they would feel free to do whatever. We experimented on just about every drug that was available to us. I began to learn how to get high and to come down quickly enough before my mother came home. I am not sure if she ever suspected anything, but if she did I guess she was too tired from work to deal with it. Not only did my friends and I do drugs together, but we found ways to obtain alcohol and we had our fun. In all honestly I never liked the taste or smell of alcohol, but pretended to enjoy it for their sake.

Being left alone made me yearn for company so I did whatever it took to keep from being alone. I was fifteen when I hooked up with my first boyfriend. He was twenty. I met him at a party. I frequently went to parties on Saturday nights because my mother was working. He was my secret. Only one or two of my friends knew about him, but that was it. I never mentioned him to my mother or my father.

I was sixteen when we first got together sexually. I was afraid and knew in my conscience I should not be with him, but I longed for friendship and company especially from a man. He asked me if it was okay. My mind said no, but my lips said yes. Our sexual relationship followed a set routine. He knew my mother's schedule just as much as I did and he would come to the house when she was at work. It lasted for about six months until a neighbor of mine got a little concerned and called the police. That night my boyfriend was a little more drunk than usual and he was hurting me a bit. I guess I made too much noise because the police were at the door. And all I can say is the rest is history.

When the police found out I was sixteen and he was twenty it became the court case of the city. I was never so embarrassed in my life. I could barely look at my mother let alone speak to her. My father came from Lusk and spent a whole month with us. He blames himself and of course my mother blames herself. The whole school couldn't stop talking behind my back. At that moment I had made up in my mind to make sure I do my best in school so I could receive all the scholarships needed to go to a college far away from Riverton.

After leaving Riverton I have never returned. I attended the University of Maine at Farmington and later moved to Atkinson, New Hampshire. I have plans of returning to Riverton to see my mother. She is ill and I would hate to not see her before she dies, but there is a part of me that feels nothing but shame just thinking about returning to Riverton.

Allison K.

Village of Shorewood, Wisconsin

When I was seven years old I was adopted by a gay couple. I really didn't understand the concept, but I was happy to be living in a home and not at an adoption agency. They were really nice to me and treated me very well. I never wanted for anything. I guess you can say I was spoiled. However, there was always a part of me that wondered where my biological parents were. I would ask on occasion, but neither one of my dads would answer me. After being ignored I began to become that loud wheel. You know, the one that gets the most attention.

I would ask about my parents more frequently and would ask if we could go to the adoption agency and figure out where they are. Finally, after much reservation my dads caved in and took me to the agency. To my surprise my biological parents lived not too far away from me, but had signed papers stating they didn't want to see me; that hurt. However, through dogged research I found both my grandparents and without my dads' knowledge sought them out. Both sets of grandparents were happy to meet me. Through them I found out the truth about my parents. It was a truth that I did not want to know. Both my parents did not want a child at the time...the condom broke. I never in my life felt so unwanted and angry. My self-esteem was shot down to the ground, not that it was far from it in the first place, but I now wished I would have listened to my dads and left my real parents unknown.

I began to be reckless and on purpose. I felt like I had no reason to live. About a year later I broke the news to my dads. They were upset that I went behind their backs, but at that moment I didn't care anymore. I did not care about life or them or anyone. I just wanted everyone to feel the same pain I was feeling consistently on a daily basis. Wanting to do to them what they did to me.

I did not have the courage to visit them. I would follow them secretly and do nasty little things like puncture their car tires or leave garbage at their front door. I was angry. They were still married, but had no children. So apparently they never wanted children. They just abandoned me like I was garbage. I never knew how deep the pain was until I began to consciously make terrible decisions. I was seventeen and I seduced this schoolboy, which was very easy. I told him I was on the pill, but I knew I wasn't. To his surprise ten months later he was a father. He asked me if I was going to keep it, but I always skated around the question because I didn't want him to know what I had in mind.

A month after having the baby I ran away from home and ended up in a town called Murdock, Minnesota. I found an adoption agency and dropped off my baby girl. I told them that I was too young to care for it and that my parents didn't want to take care of her. I lied to them about my situation and even where I was from.

I left the agency and returned home. My parents were disappointed in me for some time after I told them what happened, but I didn't care. For whatever reason there was a part of me that enjoyed what I did. I felt free to be the one to abandon instead of being abandoned.

It was about a year later that I began to feel depressed again about my real parents. I started to think of how good I felt to leave my daughter in Murdock, that I thought the only way to feel good was to do it again. So, I went to a local bar one night and went home with a married man. It was simple to lure him into bed. I convinced him that I was fixed and that I could not have children. It was easy because he was more than drunk.

I never told him I was pregnant. My dads however were livid that I was pregnant again. I didn't tell them who it was that impregnated me. They think it was a boy I met from out of town.

This time I decided to travel to Michigan. Amadore is where I ended up. I did the same thing as the last time and left my baby. I can't explain the high I felt from doing that. At this point I was getting older and decided to live on my own. My fathers were not pleased with the choices I was making and I didn't care. I knew if I wanted to keep getting high off of abandonment I had to be alone.

I moved to Vinton, Iowa where I met this boy who said he loved me, but I never believed it. The first few times with him I didn't get pregnant because he insisted on wearing condoms. It was soon that I got the idea to puncture his condom as I was putting it on him. I don't think he realized what I had done. It was about six weeks later that I knew I was pregnant. I was afraid of what he might say so I moved to Sumner, Iowa. I left my third baby at an adoption agency in Sumner and soon moved to Wilton, Iowa.

I was starting to get tired of my actions and the high wasn't so good anymore so I thought that it was time to stop. In Wilton I met this guy who I couldn't help but get with so I did. This was the only time I had no intentions of getting pregnant, but I did. I knew that I didn't want the baby, but I knew I didn't want to go through another ten months of pregnancy so I got the idea to "accidentally" fall down the stairs. When I went to the doctor's office not only did I have to wear a cast (I broke my arm), but the two-month old fetus was declared dead.

The good I felt inside was pure evil, but I could not shake it. I found a new high and I was confused as to whether or not do it again. To make a very long story short, after three more moves, two more miscarriages, and an abortion I ended up in jail for killing my eighth born child.

When I had her I did not know what to do with her. My only thought was to kill it. I tried to make it look like an accident, but those damn detectives knew how to detect. I am now in a facility for insane people. I receive counseling every day and wish I could have been born to parents who actually wanted me, because then there is a high percentage that my life story could have been different.

Jonathan Y.

Laurel, Montana

Unlike most people I do not visit my family much. I still have a difficult time forgiving them for what they have done to me. And it is not the fact of what they have done, but the fact that they have never acknowledged it nor apologized. I have two brothers, a father, and an absent mother. My mom was a drug addict. She's clean now, but sometimes I think it's too late. I barely saw her growing up because she constantly bounced in and out of jail and rehab. So I was raised by my father who was a lawyer and spent most of his time in courtrooms or his office. My brothers are older than me, I'm the youngest. So basically everything I know or learned I learned it from them.

When I was ten years old my oldest brother who was seventeen introduced me to sex. We were alone at home and he was watching a porn video he had gotten from a friend of his. He was watching a scene of a woman performing fellatio on a man and he asked me if I knew what that felt like and I answered no. He then got us both naked and that day was my first sexual experience. After that day I was sexually active with my brother at least once a week until I was about seventeen. While he was away at college the only time I was with him was when he came home for spring, winter, and summer break.

When I was eleven my other brother who was fourteen started having sex with me and there were times when we had threesomes. Many times. It started to feel "natural" and I began to look forward to it. The only reason why I began to enjoy it was because I was told to. When I told my dad what was going on I was about twelve years old. My father simply said, just sit back and enjoy the pleasure of it, because it won't last long. I was shocked by his response, but thought it was okay being that my father said it. Although I was cleared by my father there was still a part of me that knew it was wrong so I never shared what was going on with anyone in my family or my friends. I wanted to tell my mother, but she was never sober or home enough for me to tell her.

I was seventeen when the sex ended with my oldest brother and nineteen when the sex ended with my other brother. The thing that makes me the angriest is when we get together. I am now thirty and any time we get together I feel like I went through the pain alone. Both my brothers are married with children and I cannot understand how they could just get married and have children as if none of this ever happened. I do everything I can to not see them because there is a part of me that wants to molest my brother's children as revenge. I believe my father thinks what we did was okay because we were children.

My mother doesn't even have a clue what happened. Every time I look at my brothers I stare them in the eyes, but they look away. I think they are too ashamed and fearful to talk about it. I guess they feel if you don't talk about it then you don't have to deal with it, but I cannot live another day pretending this never happened. I have been to counseling and it seems to help, but until my family can face facts I think it might be best to never see them again. I try my best to forgive my mother because I blame her the most. I feel like if she would have been sober enough she could have saved me.

Dianna U.

Eddyville, Oregon

My grandmother felt really bad as she was dying. I thought it was just physical pain, but it was more guilt and shame pain than physical. I went to visit her in the hospital and she told me she was holding on to some truth that she could not hold on to any longer. I was confused as she began to talk only because I didn't know if she or the meds were talking. She said the family had a dark and dirty secret, but she believed that I had every right to know the truth. My grandmother then said everyone should know who their real father is; in fact, it is their right to know. She began to talk about why she never agreed with artificial insemination and that it was of the devil. Every child, she told me very emphatically, should know where they come from and that should never be a secret.

I wasn't sure where she was going with all of this, but before she fell asleep she did say, "Your father is not your daddy, he is just a good man who did what was right."

She never regained consciousness and about a week later we had her funeral. I didn't tell anyone about what happened, but I couldn't shake what she'd said off of me. I had to know what she was talking about. I had to know what she was trying to tell me. I secretly tried to find out for myself who my father was, but all the papers and documents had my **father's name on it**; the man who my grandmother said is not my father. I then got the idea to hire a private detective, but I knew I didn't have the cash for that.

About two months later I finally got the courage to come clean and approach my mother. I told her what my grandmother told me and I could tell that my grandmother was not making anything up. Just by the response my mother made with her face and body told me that the man I had thought was my father is not. She told me that she couldn't tell me just yet and that I had to wait until she was ready. She then told me not to ask my father.

Three more months passed and I continued my life as if the previous events had never happened. I tried my best to forget about it, but it just would not leave me alone. I then decided to dishonor my promise and ask my father. I approached him and had this knowing feeling that he would indeed tell me.

In 1990 my mother's brother was sent to the Persian Gulf to fight in the war. He returned before it was over due to him going AWOL. They said he went crazy after witnessing his partner die in a shootout along with killing a child not realizing he was a child. When he returned home he was incoherent and did not know who he was. My mother took him in because she felt obligated being that he was her brother. The doctors told her he belonged in a mental ward, but my mother would not admit him to one.

To make a long story short, after my mother was raped by her brother, she sent him to a mental hospital and nine months later I was born. My mom's boyfriend assumed the position of dad and about two years later they married. They all agreed never to tell me the truth, but I guess the guilt was eating my grandmother alive. My real father does not know I exist. He is doing much better, but still lives in the mental hospital. It's crazy because now that I know the truth I actually wish my grandmother had never said anything. This is one piece of truth I'd rather not know.

Kevin D.

Leon, Kansas

I'll be honest I never thought that I would be well enough to exit rehab. I never thought that I would be strong enough to fight the urges of getting high. I enjoyed just about every drug out there. After clubbing and hanging out with the entirely wrong crowd I was introduced to so many drugs. However, that's not where my habits began. My mother smoked cigarettes and my father was an alcoholic. My father left all of his alcohol in easy reach and never stopped me from having a taste. My first drink was at the age of thirteen and when I got caught at fourteen he simply said, "Save me some." My mother smoked about a half a pack of cigarettes a day. When I got my first job at sixteen, in order for me to get cigarettes I would have to give my mother half my paycheck.

She would say, "If you're gonna smoke my cigs than you have to pay for them." After being taught in school not to smoke, drink, and do drugs I knew what I was doing was wrong, but my parents didn't care and even encouraged it. When I left for college, drinking and smoking was second nature for me; my first nature was walking and talking. It wasn't until a wild frat party that I had my first ecstasy pill. It was wild I tell you. I couldn't believe how high I felt. It was amazing. All **seven years of college were** parties and drugs. I almost didn't graduate. It was in college that I found out about heroin and cocaine.

When I graduated I got a job DJing at a club where drugs were all around me. Some nights I tried my best to stay completely sober, but most nights I was high as a kite. I also got introduced to mushrooms, opium, and PCP while I was at the club. I spent my nights making the best music ears can hear and getting so high that there were some nights I thought for sure I was going to die.

After leaving the club I got a job stripping at a gay bar. It sounds crazy, but stripping made more money and I needed the money to fund my high.

I first experienced marijuana at the house of a gay guy I went home with. I also had my first and last gay sexual experience that night. The high on PCP is what got me there and the high from the weed is what kept me there. It wasn't until I blacked out about a week after and woke up in the hospital that I decided it was time to end this affair with the pharmaceutical business. I spent three years in rehab and had no intentions of leaving. I was too afraid that I could not be fixed and getting out would only make me end up addicted again or even dead.

My counselor told me that I had to deal with my past. It wasn't until rehab that I realized the hatred I harbored for my parents for not having structure in our home. I blamed them for my addictions and it was my excuse for getting high. I would always tell myself that I am addicted and it's their fault. I can't control myself, but it's not my fault. After much crying and screaming I had realized it was up to me to change my habits. After meeting with my parents at the rehab and expressing to them how I felt I received the release I needed to change my habits.

After coming home from rehab I realized that I could not go back to my old jobs. Having majored in business, I decided to start my own business in counseling. As the founder and owner of Once an Addict Now I'm Sober (OAANIS) I counsel men, women, and children daily and help people release themselves from addictions.

Nathaniel C.

Malaga, Kentucky

When I was born I was considered a "mistake." My mother was the mistress of a man who claimed to be divorcing. I was originally supposed to be aborted, but my mother couldn't do it. After I was born, my father, although he had a wife and family (three children), raised me just as well. Everything I know about me and the incident is from many nights and days of overhearing conversations. When I was five, my father divorced his wife, and left his family to live with my mother. He still provided for his children and former wife and even visited them. He basically lived with two families and did so as if it was the norm; for whatever reason we continued to live as such and never really talked about the wrong in the situation.

Not only us, but our relatives who I guess were too afraid and ashamed to bring up the situation never talked about the fact that my father had two wives and fathered children from both. It was kind of like a Mormon family, however, we weren't Mormons. Growing up I did see my siblings, but it was clear that they didn't want to have anything to do with me. Their small gestures and comments always kept me unwanted and I only got along with them do to my mother's wishes.

When I was about 10 or 11 years old, according to the suicide letter I was the reason my siblings' mother killed herself. The family was never the same. Oh, they still pretended like nothing was wrong, but the tension in the air was much stronger than before. As I grew older I began to hate myself even more and wanted to die. I never wanted (I don't think anyone does) to be the object of everyone's anger and bitterness. I obviously never had any control over how I was born and I do not understand why my family cannot accept that.

Once I went to college I never attended another family function. My mother was always telling me how I should keep in contact because you never know when one of them might die. Personally, I couldn't care less if they did. They never accepted me as their own and they probably never will, so, whatever. I will admit there is a part of me that wants them to accept me as their own, because I am. I may only have half of their blood, but I still have some. I always felt half and not whole knowing they never completely loved me. I got the love I needed from both my parents, but it was never enough. It was never enough to fill my tank of acceptance and being wanted.

And of course there is a part of me that feels guilty for the death of my siblings' mother. I know I am not to blame, but the pain I feel just never goes away. It stays with me and the rejection my siblings display towards me doesn't help. I try to live past the pain, but it always draws me back. It draws me back into deep depression. I wake up crying, go to sleep crying, I even cry because I'm crying.

Many people say there is nothing like the love your family can give you. That is true, but there is nothing like the pain they give out too. It hurts the most. Every day I wish I could have been born to a married couple, one man and one woman living the way God wanted us to. But no one ever gets to choose their family. I am now living far away from my family and do not care to ever see them again. I send my parents cards and letters, but I cannot return to where I came from.

There is just too much pain there.

Yvonne E.

Cedar Fort, Utah

My father loved me and my mom. He really did, but he had issues. Issues he was too weak to deal with. I don't know what they were, but I know they had to be great enough for him to treat my mother the way he did. He had a schedule. Most men just do it without notice, but he had a schedule. Twice a day every day my mother got hit. It started out as small hits, but year after year it escalated from hits, to slaps, to punches, to kicks, to using weapons. It got worse each year but she just took it. I don't really know if my dad knew I existed or if he knew who I was. He barely made contact with me. Sometimes I don't think he even realized I was in the room. I think her body got so used to the abuse that it didn't hurt her anymore.

She would even heal from her bruises much faster as the years went by. As time went by, she acquired so much experience in concealing her bruises with make-up that she could have easily gotten a job in theater make-up. It became her. She became this woman who accepted her husband beating her. I am not sure if anyone she knew was aware of what was happening, but as for my memory no one she knew tried to stop it. I basically spent my childhood watching her go through this abuse not knowing if I should call the police or not. I was thirteen years old when I guess she finally decided that enough was enough. She secretly bought a gun and she packed me and herself up and left. I don't know what she was thinking, but my dad found us within three days. He tried to get her to come with her, but instead all I remember is a gunshot and my father falling to the ground. People nearby heard it and the police were soon on the way. The city tried to put my mother away for murder, but I would not let it happen. I watched her live her life in a prison of abuse and I was not about to let her live in a cell for the rest of her life. She ended up going to jail for nine years of her life and I hated my father for every one of those years. I blamed him because if he had not been so abusive she would have never shot him.

I hate it when people get too nosey and into people's business. My mother never deserved prison time. She never intended to kill her husband, but was merely defending herself. All people see are the outcomes, but they themselves did not experience the pain that caused those outcomes. My mother is out now and a free woman, but neither one of us will ever be free from our past. It can never be changed and just the simple fact that I witnessed the abuse my mother went through and the death of my father I really do not know if I can ever be a whole person again. I have love and respect to give, but I have still yet to truly trust anyone in my life. Always afraid they will disappoint me the way my father did. I am always checking on people and on the defensive ready to fight just in case. I feel like a scared little prey making sure my predators are nowhere around me not realizing that there is a chance that I do not have any.

But there is still the part of me that will not rest thinking better safe then sorry. It's better to keep my defenses up ready to fight, than to trust someone and get beaten. I am single and probably will stay single. No matter what ethnicity, fat, tall, thin, short, gray haired or brown haired, any time I see a man I see my father and I cannot help but to think any moment I will do something that will cause them to snap and attack me the way my father attacked my mother. I don't understand why I had to live my life the way I did, but it has taught me to at least appreciate the good times. For me they were so few, but I made sure to cherish them as they came.

Brian J.

Witten, South Dakota

The way I grew up was considered normal until I got out into the real world and found out that it was anything but normal. I had a dad and there were four women who lived in the house, but only one of them was my mother. I had a sister and a brother from my mother and a total of eight siblings from the other three women. My mother had three children, two of the other women had two and the third had four children. We all lived in the same house and there was a part of me that knew we were living incorrectly. All my friends had one dad a mom and no more than four siblings. So living the way I did I noticed the major differences. I would ask my father all the time why we lived differently, but he would always say we don't live differently, they do.

I could never believe that because it was hard to believe that out of everyone I know we were the only ones living the way we did. I was befuddled because I wasn't sure if I was supposed to follow in my father's footsteps and live the way he was living. I personally wanted to live with one woman and minimal children -- the way my friends were living. The grass just looked greener.

I could never invite my friends over because my father was afraid of their reactions. He said he didn't care about their reaction, but thought it'd be best that they didn't know. It always seemed to me he knew he was living wrongly, but didn't want to admit it or have anyone find out. Every now and then I would approach my mother and ask her questions, but she would just say this is what we believe in. I never knew why we believed in a different system, but we did and I hated it. I felt distant from the world, my friends, and even my family. I never did meet any of my relatives, because I am sure they were not in agreement with how we were living.

When I was about fourteen my father told me it would be soon that I would have to move out because a house with more than one man was not a good thing. So I prepared to leave. I got my first job and a part of me was happy and ready to leave. When I was sixteen I witnessed my sister from another mother give birth to her first child and my father's twelfth child. At that moment there was nothing anyone could tell me anymore. I knew we were living incorrectly and abnormally. I knew what we were doing was wrong, but I didn't know where to go or who to tell. When I turned seventeen my father told me I had less than a year to figure out where I was going. Without his help I decided to scholarship my way to college so that I could leave his household forever.

During my four years in college I lied about my parents and siblings, but I still knew (wasn't sure how) that I was going to rescue my siblings from that atmosphere. I got my own place and I made surprise visits (when I knew Dad was away) and slowly but surely convinced my siblings (from the same mother) to move in with me. It wasn't long before I decided to convince all my siblings to move in with me.

My father hated everything that I was doing, but I didn't care. I began to give them knowledge that our father kept from us and soon one by one each of them denounced our way of living. Each one of my siblings also began to move out, going into college, others just living on their own. I thought I was helping, but in some ways I was not.

I didn't realize the mental issues we all had considering we lived most of our lives believing how we were living was okay. One of my siblings moved back in with my father while the others went crazy; each holding on to an addiction to cope with our past lives.

After three to four years of a horrible roller coaster ride of life I decided to confront my father. By then he had fifteen children (the last three were mothered by three of my sisters). I hated him and this disgusting way of living. So I knew the only thing to do to end this was to report him. I am not sure what I was thinking, but I was just desperate to end his belief system. He was arrested for having multiple wives as well as incest and endangerment of a child (all of my sisters had their children at the age of fifteen or sixteen). I didn't realize what I was doing not just to him, but to his family. All of his wives were dependent on him so when he was arrested they had no clue how to survive without him. I did my best in teaching them how the real world functions, but they were too brainwashed to understand. They all ended up living with one of their children.

It was a press mess as they wrote every article with every pun title. My siblings were hateful towards me because they felt like I had embarrassed the family by exposing our father. I can truly say there was a side of me that wished I would have kept it all a secret, but to this day I am happier that he was exposed than I am embarrassed.

It has now been over thirty years since the incident. My mother and the other mothers have finally figured out how to live without my dad. He is out of jail with a new family hiding in Texas. My mom got remarried along with the other mothers. All my siblings are out on their own some single and others living the nuclear family lifestyle. The only thing I regret about the entire situation is that there are still families who live the way we used to and still believe that it is okay. I don't know about anyone else who lives the way I used to, but it messed me up. I am better now, single, and waiting to meet the right "one" woman.

Sandra P.

Easton, Connecticut

I thought I knew my husband. I thought I loved him until I realized I didn't know him. You never know how much you don't love someone until you realize how much you don't know about them. He was an evil man. He still is. At least he's in jail now, but I also blame myself. I am not sure why I was so blind. I didn't see any signs of anything. My husband, my ex-husband spent his Saturdays with our children. I thought it was a wonderful thing. All fathers should spend time with their children. I just didn't know what he was doing with them.

We had four children, two girls and two boys. They were beautiful. Three of them have passed away and the last one alive is in a psych ward. She doesn't belong there though.

My husband who is in jail now would take our children to this place I would never allow him to take them if I had known what was going on. There was this place, an underground place, a place where they would make money selling children for sex. My husband would make lots of money allowing them to use our children. He would, according to my children, take them there and they would each be escorted to a separate room and for hours he would wait in the waiting room as men and women would pay to have sex with them.

When police found out about the place my ex was sent to jail. My children along with the other children testified against the people who owned the place and even the regulars. Over one hundred of them ended up in jail for Endangerment of a Child; many of them on multiple counts. I thought I was in a nightmare and couldn't wake up. After the case was over I began to slowly try to talk to my children, but they were all messed up by then. My oldest son went off to war. He was never the fighting kind, but he was just trying to get away. He died in Iraq. My oldest daughter became a full-time prostitute and was killed by a pimp or client, I am not too sure of the story.

I just wanted to die. I really wanted to kill my ex-husband. He was the cause of this mess. Last, but not least my youngest son couldn't live with the pain so he ended his life with a bottle of Advil. My last child and youngest went crazy and ended up in a mental hospital. I can't do anything anymore. I try to continue my life, but I feel I am the one who ended it. Not once did I suspect anything. Not once did I think something was wrong with my children. I never in a million years thought anything of the sort was happening to my children.

I spent years hating that man. The man I thought I knew, the man I thought I loved. There is a part of me that wishes I would have listened to the voice inside of me that said not to marry him. But I thought I was so in love. It is so strange how knowledge can change the feelings you thought you had for someone. Simple knowledge can change your trust into distrust, your respect into disrespect, and your love into hate. And it is not just the knowledge, but it's coming into the knowledge.

I loved that man all the years he was defiling my children, but it wasn't until I came into the knowledge that I realized I never loved him. Why is that? Why is it that you get to the point where it is too late that you realize the truth? I wish I would have known what kind of man he was before I got married. I blame myself daily and in contradiction tell myself it is not my fault. I really wish I could have seen or heard something early on to stop the pain my ex-husband inflicted on his own children. Our children. But of course it is just too late.

Lisa M.

Hartford, Alabama

Many people who know my family believe it should not be. Those who forget mercy and forgiveness always tell me I am living the wrong way. My story begins when I was twenty-five years old. I married a man I should not have married. We were more than opposites. We never agreed on anything, but I was desperate to get away from my current life and he promised me he could do that. We were married for three years and then my crazy life began. One night I was making my normal beer run for my husband and the craziest most unimaginable thing happened. On the way home I was raped by a man who apparently was a novice at the whole game of raping. He spoke to me and he showed his face and did not kill me.

When I got home my husband was more concerned about the beer than me. I pressed charges and gave a description of the man. He was arrested and charged with rape. Nine months later I gave birth to his son. My husband was disgusted that I decided to give birth to a rape baby. He told me to abort it, but I couldn't. When my son was about six months my husband took him out to what I thought was a birthday party of his boss' son. To my surprise he returned home without my son. He simply told me he couldn't have a rape baby in the house so he gave my son up for adoption.

I felt paralyzed and I am not sure why. I allowed him to control me in every way. There I was, I could have run, but I stayed. I thought about my son every day. Wondering if he was put in a good home or not. Everything in me told me to go get my son back, but I felt afraid.

Five years after the incident I got a divorce and moved out. There was a part of me that wanted to look for my son, but I was too afraid to and I am not sure why. About a year had passed before I came to the conclusion that I will not spend another year, month, week, or day without my son. I then began looking and searching for my son. I went to every adoption agency, foster care, and anything else I could think of. A year later I found my son. Thankfully he was adopted by a single man who worked in the adoption agency. Apparently none of the families he was put with wanted him. They said he was non-social and unwanted. The man at the adoption agency felt badly so he decided to adopt my son. My son was eight years of age when I found him. I made a deal with his adopted father if I could be in his life without him knowing who I was. I didn't know how to explain to him just yet what

happened. His father agreed and for the next three

years I became Aunt Lisa.

For whatever reason I decided that the man who raped me should know that he has a son. I found out what prison he was in and I visited him. Surprisingly, he remembered me; he even apologized and told me he never wanted to hurt anyone. He said he was used to abusing women because his father did. However, he said he knew he wasn't his father and was glad he was caught. He told me his jail time had changed him and he knew he was a changed man. Finally, I told him why I was there and he was shocked. I gave him a picture of his son and he cried. He was happy, yet angry at how his son was conceived. I remember when he looked at the picture and said, "I sure as hell can't deny this child."

His son had the same green eyes and orange hair as he did. To be honest they were both beautiful people. I personally just felt like he should know he has a son. He began to ask me questions about him and we talked for some time. I soon finished the conversation and was on my way. Before I left he asked me to come back and visit. I was shocked and speechless. I really didn't know what to say. Saying yes would be crazy, but I didn't want to say no. I know what he did to me, but I will say the man I talked to in the prison was not the same man who raped me. He spent a total of thirteen years in prison and from the first time I spoke to him to the day he got out I visited him, in secret of course. When he got out he wanted to meet his son, but there was no way of explaining him to our son. He was the spitting image of his father and unless our son was completely stupid there was no way to deceive him into thinking this man was not his father. I talked to his adoptive father and he was not in agreement. I continued to see my son, but his father was not permitted. I would bring to his father videos and pictures so he could see his son.

When our son turned fifteen as crazy as it sounds me and his father got married. Sometimes I feel like all things happen for a reason. He was everything I needed in a spouse and yet he was the man who raped me. We tried to keep our relationship a secret, but it was getting more difficult every day. I remember when my son turned sixteen he saw his father and me at the supermarket. He didn't show himself, but he asked his father who the man was. Because my son realized for himself who the man was there was no lying.

We sat him down and explained to him the entire story. It was difficult for the next three years. He had many questions and found it difficult to forgive me and his father for lying to him. The three of us now communicate with each other on a daily basis. Although my son is twenty-one years young and it feels like it is too late, me and his father still consider ourselves to be his parents. We meet for dinner, go to the movies, and continue to live like a regular family. His adoptive father still has legal custody, but we don't let the law stop us from living as a family.

Our son is in college now and is an advocate against rape and speaks to high schools and college communities about the importance of reporting rape and talking to young men to learn how to accept no. It may sound like an unlikely story, but I didn't choose it. I just lived it.

Conclusion

First and foremost, I would like to thank all those who shared their lives with me. Living has taught me that everyone has dysfunctions in their family. However, there are two different types of people; those who mope about their dysfunctions and those who use them to better their and other's lives. I have decided to share these essays to show you that you are not the only one going through difficult, crazy, weird, abnormal, and dysfunctional times. We all are and we can either complain and judge, or confess and share with each other and then help each other to overcome. I hope this book encourages you to share your story instead of hiding it. May you have peace and comfort.

Dean Kyle Brent

No matter where you come from, where you lived, whether wealthy or poor, black or white, fat or thin, everyone has lived in a dysfunctional family. And that's what this book brings light to. Dean Brent has put together stories from lives not afraid to share their dysfunctional family story. This book not only encourages you to appreciate your life, but to realize that everyone is born into a dysfunctional family, but no one has to stay in one. Reading this book has encouraged me to deal with the dysfunctions in my family and to not just ignore them, but to repair them. anyone anywhere who has a family MUST read this book.

Dr. Reginald Denny, PhD.

Dean Kyle Brent is the first time author of, "Essays from Dysfunctional Families." This manuscript won first place in the Writers' FORUM Fiction Competition, which led to the publication of this book. Dean is originally from Deming, New Mexico, USA.

LITERARY BETRAYAL

Casey Bell

When I was born I was considered a "mistake." My mother was the mistress of a man who was said to be divorcing. I was originally supposed to be aborted, but my mother couldn't do it. After being born my father although he had a wife and family (four children) he raised me just as well. Everything I know about me and the incident is from many nights and days of overhearing conversations. When Literary I was five, my father divorced his wife, and left his family [illegible] with [illegible] mother. He [illegible] provided for his children and former wife and even visited them. He basically lived with two families and did so as if it was the norm; for whatever reason we continued to live as such and never really talked about the wrong in the situation. Not only us, but our relatives who guessed were too afraid and ashamed to bring up the situation never talked about the fact that my father had two wives and father children from both. It was kind of like a Mormon family, however, we weren't Mormons. Growing up I did see my siblings, but it was clear that they didn't want to have anything to do with me. Their small gestures and comments always kept me unwanted and only got along with them do to my mother's wishes. When I was about 10 or 11 years old according to the suicide letter I was the reason my siblings' mother killed herself. The family was never the same. Oh, the [illegible] nothing [illegible] wrong. [illegible] the [illegible] was [illegible] than [illegible] I grew older I began to hate Betrayal myself even more and wanted to die. I never wanted (I don't think anyone does) to be the object of everyone's anger and bitterness. I never had any control over how I was born and do not understand why [illegible] that. Once I went to college I never went to another family function.

Literary Betrayal©

Casey S. Bell

Published by: BookCase Publishing

http://bookcasepublishing.weebly.com

Editor: Michael Valentine

Cover Design by CSB Printing

Printed in the United States

http://www.caseysamuelbell.com

CONTENTS

Day 1 in New Mexico

Kimberley is in the kitchen cooking a feast for herself and her husband. On the front eye of the stove to the right she is boiling a pot of mixed vegetables. On the back burner there is a pot of rice. To the left in front is a pan of salmon. Kimberly takes the pot in the back to the left and strains the potatoes. She then pours the potatoes in a bowl and mashes them adding sea salt and butter. As she continues cooking she overhears the television. She stops and puts everything down and runs to the family room. She takes the remote control and turns it up. The anchor of the five ʻo-clock news is speaking.

"The author of 'Essays from Dysfunctional Families,' will be coming to the United States for a book signing tour. The author, Dean Brent, who had his book released in London after three years is finally coming to the States. Brent is originally from Deming, New Mexico and moved to England after winning a short story contest. His short story 'Essays from Dysfunctional Families' not only won the contest, but sold worldwide in the billions being translated in over thirty languages. The book was number one on the bestseller list for many months and is still considered one of the best books ever written. The book contains ten essays by ten different people living in the United States and is said to be fiction, but there is controversy over whether or not they are based on true stories. Dean Brent has yet to return to the States since he moved to London. I am sure his fans here will be happy to see him. In other news-"

Kimberley turns off the television.

"I don't believe it. He could have at least told me he was coming."

Alerted by noises in the kitchen, she mutters, "O my goodness! My dinner."

Kimberley runs to the kitchen to finish the meal. As she continues Mark enters. He is wearing a Kenneth Cole Select Label charcoal suit with a pale blue button down dress shirt and a charcoal and pale blue striped tie. He enters, sniffing, walks into the kitchen and looks around.

"Are you burning something?"

"Well, hi to you too, honey."

"Hey Kim. How are you doing?"
he says and kisses her on the lips.

"Are you burning something?"

"No. A little. I got caught up in the television."

Mark looks into the living room and sees the television is not on.

"Babe, Hon, the television isn't on."

"I know, Honey, I just turned it off."

"Well, what was on TV that got you burning dinner?"

"It's not burnt. You'll never believe what they said."

"Try me."

"Mr. Dean Brent is visiting the good ol' US of A. Isn't that exciting news?"

Mark doesn't answer.

"Babe, did you hear me? I said Brent is finally coming home to visit us. Isn't that exciting?"

Mark stands there as if he is in flashback mode just staring off in to space.

"Mark, wake up! Do you hear me?"

"Yeah, I hear you."

"Then say something."

"What do you want me to say?"

"Gee, I don't know, maybe, wow, that is exciting; someone I love who I have not seen for three years is coming home to visit. I am so excited."

"Did you forget that Emanuel ran off to England and pretty much said he never wanted to see us again? What makes you think he's going to visit us? He's probably just doing a book signing and then leaving."

"Dean loves us. He was just upset when he said that. He's probably coming to apologize. And his name is not Emanuel anymore, it's Dean."

"Emanuel doesn't like us. I don't even think he has forgiven us. You read the book. Those stories were too familiar; especially Nathaniel C. from Malaga, Kentucky."

"All writers use their life to inspire their writings; songwriters, playwrights, screenwriters, poets, all of them."

"I just don't know what to think. He left here on bad terms."

"I don't know about you, but I know my Dean, my Emanuel, is coming to visit me. Now go get cleaned up. Dinner will be ready soon."

He inspects the pots on the stove.

"You plan on unburning it before you serve it?"

"It's not burnt!"

Day 3 in New Mexico

It has been three days since Dean Brent has entered the USA and he has yet to visit his family. He has been busy going from book store to talk shows to radio shows to bookstore talking about his arrival in the States and his bestseller. His tour began in New Mexico and will end in New Mexico. He will be visiting over a hundred bookstores, over fifty radio shows and over twenty talk shows both local and national over a six-month period. As of now he is on a local talk show, "The Good Sunshine Show," with Shelly Bellis. Kimberley is sitting in front of her television with a huge smile on her face. Although her son hasn't visited her as of yet she is still excited that he is in the States.

"So it has been three years since Mr. Dean Brent has returned. Everyone everywhere wanted to know why and if he ever planned to show his face here in America. Well, as we all know Mr. Brent will be touring for six months and our show is one of the first stops. Ladies and Gentlemen, I want you to give a warm welcome to New Mexico's own fabulous bestselling author, Mr. Dean Kyle Brent."

A loud applause in ovation is heard. Kimberley is seen wiping her tears from her face.

"I am so proud of you, Emanuel. I mean Dean. That's my baby.

As the applause continues Dean enters the stage and walks straight to Shelly and embraces her with a hug. He then bows at the audience in appreciation. He smiles, blows kisses and mouths the words, "Thank you." He soon motions the audience to quiet down and to take their seats. He sits as well as Shelly does and Shelly begins.

"So, Dean, it is nice to have you on our show."

"Thank you for inviting me."

"Oh, it's our pleasure. So, what is it like to be in your home state once again?"

"It's altogether strange. It's only been three years, but it seems like an eternity. But it's still pretty nice to be somewhere familiar."

"Do you plan on returning permanently?"

"No. I enjoy living in London. It's a great city. The people there are nice to me."

"So, how did this all happen for you? You were a New Mexican man and then all of a sudden you became a bestselling author living in London."

"Well, I was in New Mexico and I couldn't get a job. I was at the end of my rope and I saw an ad on a website about a writing competition. The prize was money, a free trip to London, and a chance to get your book published by a London Publishing company. I really had nothing to lose so I started writing the book, 'Essays from Dysfunctional Families,' and I entered the contest and the rest is history."

"What was it like when you found out that you won the contest?"

"It was exciting because I knew there was a chance that I could get the book published which meant I would have a job as an author, but at the same time I was completely shocked because I had never written a book before so I couldn't believe I actually won."

"What made you think you could write a book?"

"Well, when I was in school I had to write essays and short stories for English class and all my English teachers encouraged me to take up creative writing. They all said I had something."

"That's amazing. So what took you so long to come back to the States?"

"I don't know. I got so used to living in England that I just didn't want to leave."

"Did the lawsuit have anything to do with you not wanting to come back?"

"Oh, Shelly, you sure know how to ask the right questions."

"I'm sorry. Was that too much of a tough question?"

"No, I'm just kidding. No, the lawsuit had nothing to do with it."

"Talk to us about the lawsuit. I mean we have heard everyone's side of the story. I would like to hear yours?"

"Well, the man, Franklin Thompson, sued me for plagiarism."

"Right, was it true though? Because as it ended you signed an agreement to pay him a certain amount of money."

"Yeah, sorta, kinda. The essays in the book are all based on true events. The story of Kevin D was based on Franklin's life. Frank thought that it was wrong that I used his life without his permission. In a sense he was right. That's why I didn't allow him to take me to court. I just paid him his dues and the publishers added his name to the credits in the book."

"How did you meet Franklin?"

"I met him in school. We were roommates in college for two semesters. A lot of the things added in Kevin D's story were fabricated, but the story itself was based on Franklin."

"That's fascinating. So, it's been three years and where is the sophomore book?"

"I don't know. I haven't been able to think of anything that could follow the success of 'Essays from Dysfunctional Families.' It really seems to be a great book not only in England and the United States, but in many other countries."

"Let's talk about that. The book was translated in over thirty languages, how did that make you feel?"

"It was amazing. I couldn't believe it when I heard it myself. I just felt really blessed to know many people from different countries would be reading this book."

"So how do you know whether or not they translated your book correctly?"

"Oh, I don't know. It's just a trust thing. I have to trust the translators did their job to the best of their ability."

"So what was your sole purpose of even deciding to write this particular book?"

"Well, as I said I was mainly just trying to win a contest to get out of debt. But I also wanted to free people of thinking that there is such a thing as a perfect family. Many people always live thinking their family is the only family with dysfunctions. But I wanted to show lives of different people living in different places going through different situations in their life, but still all of them went through the same thing which is surviving a dysfunctional family.

"Lots of times we think we are to blame for living in such messed up families, but we don't get to choose how we are born, but we do get to choose how we are going to grow from our situations and issues."

"Wow, that is magnificent. If I be honest after reading this book I cried for days. It was about a month later that I went to my family and I confessed everything I was hiding and came clean before my parents."

"That's good. And that's what I wanted; people clearing themselves of their secrets."

"Amazing. So do you have any plans while you are in your home state?"

"Not really. Nothing spectacular."

"Nothing, really? Well, I hope you enjoy the next months being in the good ol' US of A. We want to thank Dean for coming on our show."

The audience cheers loudly.

Dean responds, "Thank you."

"Coming up next on the Good Sunshine Show, have you been feeling pains in your body? Next up is Dr. Riley Bean. He will be telling us what those pains could be telling you about your health. Don't go away."

Kimberley turns off the television in dismay a little disappointed.

"He said nothing. I cannot believe he would come all this way and not even pay a visit."

A disappointed silence follows.

"He said nothing."

Day 5 in New Mexico

Dean is standing by a shelf in a supermarket. He is holding a can of pickles and reading the back.

"Why do they have to put high fructose corn syrup in everything? I guess I have to get organic," he murmurs to himself.

As he stands there looking through the pickle brands a woman notices him. She tries to get a look at his face making sure he is who she believes he is. After some time, she walks towards Dean.

"Excuse me."

Dean looks at the woman and responds, "Yes."

After seeing him she shrieks. Dean says, "Ma'am, are you okay?"

"Oh my goodness, I cannot believe it is you. You are Dean Brent."

"Yes, I am."

She shrieks again, "Oh my! Can I touch you?"

"Sure, I guess."

She hesitantly touches him and then shrieks again.

Dean just stands making faces that speak: this is a weird woman.

"Mr. Brent, let me just tell you I love your book. After reading it I bought a whole bunch of copies for my family, friends, and co-workers. I just had to share it with everyone. You do not know what you have done to me by writing that book."

"Well, I am happy you enjoyed it."

"Enjoyed it? I did more than just enjoyed it. You saved my life and the life of so many others. I was able to free myself of the dysfunction I was born into and finally realize that I was not at fault for the craziness life I had to live. You taught me that it's okay to be born in a dysfunctional family, but it's not okay to stay in one."

"Well, I'm glad you learned that."

The woman continues, "Let me tell you something I grew up in a messed up family. When I was growing up my dad was a Jewish Nazi and my mother was a Catholic pastor who would preach down at the Methodist church not far from our home. She would preach to my dad about Jesus and my dad would tell her to shut up. It just didn't make any sense to me why they ever got married in the first place. Let me tell you I was one messed up girl. But after reading your book I am changed woman. I have come to realize we are not our parents, we **are not** our family, and we are not our relatives. We can truly come into our own and be our own person. I just want to thank you for sharing those essays. If you write another one don't be afraid to use my story. I won't be mad at you. And I won't sue you either. Sharing our lives is what we need to do. Thank you Dean Brent. Thank you so much Dean Kyle Brent."

"You're welcome."

She stares at Dean with a huge appreciative smile. He just stands there uncomfortable not sure how to respond. The woman then grabs Dean and embraces him with a tight bear hug. Dean just receives it in hopes it will end soon. The woman lets go of Dean and smiles.

"Thank you, Dean. I love you, man."

"You're welcome."

The woman walks away and Dean just watches her walk away in complete amazement.

"This is why I was not excited about returning. They don't even let you shop."

Dean finally takes a jar of organic pickles and continues shopping. As he walks down another aisle another woman notices him and she looks at him seeing if he is who she believes he is. She finally approaches Dean.

"Excuse me."

Dean whispers to himself, "Not again."

He turns towards the woman and pauses. He just looks at her in amazement and not really sure how to respond. The woman asks, "Emanuel?"

"Yeah, it's me."

"My, God, Manny! Do you recognize me?"

"Karen."

"So, you haven't forgotten."

She embraces him and he returns the embrace.

"Everyone said that after you moved to London you forgot us all, but I knew you wouldn't forget me. It's so great to see you. So, what are you doing here?"

"I'm doing a book signing tour."

"Really? Why didn't you tell anyone you were returning? Absolutely no one is talking about it?"

"It's all over TV, the radio, newspapers. I thought everyone knew."

"I don't do that stuff. Manny, you should have made a formal announcement. I can't believe I am looking at you. I honestly thought you were gone for good."

Dean speaks under his breath, "So did I."

"So how long are you staying?"

"I'm doing a six-month American tour. I leave New Mexico for Texas in about a week."

"Well, we have to get together before you leave. We haven't seen each other in over three years. I want to get to talk to you before you leave for good. I know you have no plans of coming back here."

"Well, I'm staying at the Holiday Inn, room 515. I'll be in my room tonight after nine. Just come on over and knock."

"That'll be great. I'll see you there."

Dean is sitting in bed in his hotel room. He has a bunch of papers on his bed that he is looking over. A knock sounds at the door. His conscience tells him who it is. He nervously freezes, unaware of the outcome. He finally comes to his senses and puts his paperwork away. After another knock he finally runs to the door and cautiously opens it.

"Hey."

"Did I catch you at a bad time?"

"No, come right in."

"You said after nine, I hope this isn't too late."

"No, not at all."

"Did I wake you?"

"No, I was just going over some paperwork."

"I'm sorry. I didn't know you were working. I can come back another time."

"No, it's okay. It's not important. It can wait."

An uncomfortable silence hits the room. They look at each other waiting for the other to speak. Finally, Karen speaks up. "So, do you get to see Queen Elizabeth often?"

"Not really. I've seen her on a few occasions."

"Have you been in the palace yet?"

"No. I would have had to do something pretty special to be invited to the palace."

"You only wrote one of the best books in our nation, in our time."

"Being in England is like being in America. No one spends their time trying to see the government. If it happens then it happens."

"But England is so much different. I mean the Queen is more important than any American president."

Another silence fills the room. Dean exits the silence.

"So, how are you feeling?"

"I'm doing pretty well."

They stare at each other as silence reenters. Karen speaks. "It is really nice to see you once again. I'm really glad you turned out okay. I thought for a moment that you were going to end up__"

She pauses and stares at him some more.

"Well, I don't want to keep you from your work."

"Karen."

She stops halfway to the door, turns and looks back at him and smiles. He pauses and hesitantly goes to speak.

"I'm sorry."

She looks puzzled. "Sorry about what?"

"As if you don't know."

"What are you apologizing for?"

"I know you're upset with me, along with everyone else I know."

"What makes you think that?"

Dean pauses, then abruptly changes the subject. "Never mind. It was nice seeing you."

"Just say it, Emanuel. Why can't you just say what's on your lips, your tongue, your mouth; it's all over you?"

"Because then I'll have to-"

"You'll have to what…have to admit you were wrong?"

"Why couldn't you just accept the apology like any normal person?"

"According to your book I am not a normal person. I am from a dysfunctional family. So I might as well give a dysfunctional response."

"I don't believe that. It was just for the sake of the contest."

"How could you do that? How could you put my whole life in a book and not even consult me?"

"Honestly, I was just trying to write something that would catch the eyes of the judges."

"Why didn't you ask me before you threw it in the book?"

"Would you have said yes?"

No response gives Dean the answer

Karen speaks. "So you knew I would say no. Why would you do it knowing I would have said no?"

"I was desperate. It was my only chance at making some real money."

"You had no right adding my story to the essays."

"You know; I really knew I was wrong in all I did, but I am willing to apologize to everyone. That is the only reason why I left England so that I could apologize because I knew everyone would be angry. I just wish you all would return the favor."

"What do I need to apologize for?"

"You killed my child."

"I had a miscarriage. I can't believe you thought I miscarried on purpose all those times. And I never had an abortion. That is what angered me the most. You made me look like an evil woman. And I did not kill my last child. It was an accident. You know that. Do you seriously believe I'm that kind of a woman?"

Dean does not respond to Karen's question.

"Answer me damn it!"

"I honestly don't know what to think. What am I supposed to think, three miscarriages?"

"I had four miscarriages. None of them were on purpose and none of them were an abortion. Okay, yes I admit it; my life was fucked up, but I would not and could not do something that drastic. You made me look like I was mentally and emotionally insane and evil. Is that what you thought of me?"

Dean again slowly responds.

Karen responds angrily, "Come on, man, answer me. Is that what you thought of me?"

"Karen, the book was fabricated. A lot of it was fiction added on to the facts. Look, I am sorry for doing what I did, but at the time I thought it was my only choice of surviving. I'm surprised you didn't sue me like Franklin."

"I very well wanted to, but I feared the consequences. You painted me as a baby killer. I didn't want people knowing I was Allison K. from Village of Shorewood, Wisconsin. And what the hell was that?"

"I just wanted to share the stories. I wanted the people and where they came from to be anonymous. I thought if I fabricate the names and their locations then absolutely no one would be able to identify the real people. I had the notion that some of you may be hurt, but I…I was just desperate. I am so sorry."

"You should have never done it. You had other choices."

"What's done is done. What more do you want me to do?"

A silence hits the room before Karen breaks it. "How much money did you make from the book?"

"I should have known this was about the money. What do you want, for me to write you a check?"

"Honestly, yes. I can't shake the feeling of feeling like you got rich off my story."

"Part of it was mine."

"But most of it was mine. You got paid millions and I got paid nothing. The story was 50/50 mine and yours so the cash should be 50/50 as well."

"If you want money then money is what you will get. I will have my accountant on it the first thing in the morning."

She hands him a business card.

"There's all my information. I'm sure your accountant will need that."

Karen pauses once again, not feeling good about the situation. She continues, saying, "I never wanted it to end this way."

"Neither did I, but just like I said in my book some things you just don't get to choose. It was nice seeing you once again, Karen. Long time no see."

"Yeah, same here. Bye, Manny."

She kisses him on the lips, smiles and then walks out of the room. Dean returns to his bed and plops on it.

"I knew this was going to happen."

Day 6 in New Mexico

Dean arrives to a house that he hasn't seen in three years. Knowing the attendant's schedule and hoping it didn't change, he exits the car and walks towards the door. He goes to knock, but then places his hand at his side and stands there not sure whether or not to enter. He waits for some time and decides to knock. His heart begins to pump heavily as he waits for someone to answer the door. As the seconds roll by he becomes more nervous and begins to wish he never knocked. As he sweats inwardly the door opens. The man on the other side just stares completely shocked. Not sure how to respond neither the man nor Dean knows what to do or say. Finally, Dean opens his mouth a nervously utters, "Hi, Dad."

"Is it really you?"

"Yeah, Dad. It's me."

The man just stares not really sure how to respond to seeing his estranged son.

Dean asks, "May I come in?"

Nervously, the man says, "Well, of course. Come right in."

The man just stares at Dean not able to speak.

"Is everything okay, Dad?"

The man grabs Dean and embraces him in a long bear hug. Dean returns the hug. After some time, they release. As they return to staring at each other each man's tears flow freely. Finally, a voice is heard from upstairs. "Mark, honey, who's at the door?"

"Kimie, baby, come downstairs and find out for yourself."

"Well, you don't have to be so rude, Mark."

As she walks down the stairs she fixes herself not knowing who is in the house. As she gets closer her eyes dilate and she uncontrollably screams and attacks Dean with a hug. Once she lets go she slaps him on the butt.

"What the hell is wrong with you? Three years…three years, Manny? No phone calls, no letters, no emails, nothing."

"Mother, I am so sorry."

She grabs him again and embraces him.

"Oh, I never want to let go."

"Mom."

They release from the embrace.

"Dad, Mom, I am truly sorry for everything I have done in the past three years. Desperation can make one do some really mean things. I had no intentions on hurting anyone in the process."

Kimberley says, "Well, baby, in all honesty when you reach for success whether you mean to or not, someone is going to get hurt. It just comes with the territory. But through all that has happened I want you to know that I forgive you and I still love you."

"Thanks, Mom."

Mark says, "You know I still love you, son? For always."

"Yes, Dad, I know. I love you too."

Kim excitingly says, "Well, Manny...Dean, you came just in time. You know this Friday is our annual Fourth of July get together at Aunt Sarah's."

"Mom, I probably won't have time for that. I have radio shows, TV shows, book signings and a whole bunch of other business matters to deal with."

"Son, you haven't seen them in over three years. I think it would be rude for you to come to home and not even acknowledging them."

"Mother, I don't know."

Mark intervenes, "Son, just think about it. I'm sure they would all like to see you."

Dean hesitantly ponders, then says, "If my schedule permits I'll see what I could do."

Kim says, "That's great. My baby is back. It's gonna be like old times."

Dean responds to his mother's comment. "That may not be a good thing."

"What's that supposed to mean?"

Mark interjects, "Babe, why don't you fix him something to eat."

"Ooh, that's a great idea. I'll heat up these left-overs."

Mark says to Dean, "I hope you don't mind burnt food."

"It's not burnt," says Kimberley.

Day 9 in New Mexico

At Aunt Sarah's house, family members have surrounded a huge dinner table ready to eat. A man yells out, "How come we are not outside? It's summer."

Sarah says, "Joe, you can eat outside, but as for me I am eating inside. I don't like being around bugs."

"Then I guess you're going to have to get away from Uncle Joe."

Everyone responds with jeers and cheers.

"You keep that up, Kendra. I'll beat your smart ass. Just try me."

"I'm just messing, Uncle Joe."

Olivia says, "Somebody pass me the peas."

Johnny asks, "Did you say pass the peas?"

Olivia smiles knowing what's coming next. The family begins to sing "Pass the Peas." As they do the doorbell rings.

Aunt Sarah asks, "Well, who could that be?

"Heather, go get the door."

Heather walks towards the door pondering her hardest trying to figure out who it could be, for she knows everyone invited is already there. As she opens the door she is stunned and can't speak. Aware of the response, Dean with a little depressed tone speaks. "Hi."

"Hey, what are you doing here?"

"My mother invited me…she said I should come by. I could leave though."

"No, no, of course not. Come on in."

Heather leads him into the dining room. "Look what the dog done dragged in."

As they see Dean they all chime in with their own two cents. Mark and Kimberley sit, simply pleased their son decided to join them.

Johnny says, “Hey look, it’s good old Manny. Never thought I see you again.”

Uncle Joe interjects, “His name ain’t Manny anymore, it’s Dean now.”

Everyone laughs at the comment. Uncle Joe continues, “Well, if it ain’t the bestselling book author. Well, how you’ve been?”

“Doing, pretty well.”

“Well, that’s just good.”

Kendra says,“Doing more than well, I’m sure. How’s my favorite brother?”

Johnny says, “Excuse me?”

Robert responds, “Johnny, you heard her. And you thought it was you.”

Johnny says, “Shut up, Bobby. You always got something to say.”

"You're just upset that your brother from another mother is your sister's favorite."

Kendra chimes in, "Come on, guys, you know I'm just teasing."

Dean quietly greets everyone knowing not to respond to the conversation. He first greets his parents, Mark and Kimberley. Kimberley simply smiles at him in appreciation of Dean joining the family once again. After he greets his siblings, Johnny, Kendra, and Olivia, Dean then walks over to Mark's sister. Aunt Sarah greets him with a warm hug knowing she was the only relative who really accepted him. He next approaches Uncle Joe, Sarah's husband.

After that greets Joe and Sarah's children, his cousins, Heather and Robert. He then greets Matthew, Mark's brother, and his wife, Aunt Rachel. Lastly he greets Matthew's and Rachel's children, his cousins, Nicole and Aaron.

After much celebration from his family, that Dean is unsure is real or fake Aunt Sarah says, "Alright ya'll, make room for Manny. He's back."

Joe says, "It's about damn time. Three years and not much as a phone call or even letter. What happened out there in the Promised Land; did you forget your past?"

Sarah speaks before Dean can answer. "Now, Joe, not today. We're going to have a nice family dinner."

"Then when, tomorrow? It's not like he's gonna stay long enough for that. His plane for London probably leaves tomorrow?"

Aaron answers, "Not according to the news. He's here for six months. He's doing a book tour in the US."

Joe responds, "Oh, so this was just a convenient visit. All I know is we better watch what we say. It just might end up in another bestseller."

Rachel now says, "Joe, why do you always have to ruin things with your mouth? Can you for once just keep quiet?"

Aunt Sarah has an answer. "Joe is addicted to using his mouth for garbage. For him to shut up is like going through withdrawal for him."

Everyone responds with laughter. Sarah convenes, "Joe, just keep quiet. I want to have a peaceful dinner."

Joe continues in an English accent, "So, Manny, where's your British accent?"

Robert says, "He probably lost it with his name."

Everyone responds some with laughs, others with jeering facial expressions. Nicole asks, "Manny, why did you change your name? I always liked your name, Emanuel Reed."

Dean says, "I just thought it would be cool to have a pen name."

Joe interrupts. "Well, I think it's stupid."

Sarah speaks. "Joe, what did I just say?"

"No, babe, I need to say this. I hate it when celebrities change their name. It is just immoral. I don't care what your daddy did, you are supposed carry his name. I don't care who you are, especially if you're a man, you're supposed bear that name with pride."

Olivia asks, "Where did you get the name from? It's so peculiar, Dean Kyle Brent, what kind of name is that?"

Dean responds with a smile. "When I first got to London I was a bit scared. There were brothers who lived in an apartment room next to mine. They were very helpful in helping me get around the city. I put their names in order of birth."

Aaron asks, "What is it like being a bestselling author?"

"I haven't really thought about it yet."

Kendra speaks. "It's been three years. What's not to think about?"

"I don't know. I guess it's just not that important to me."

Joe responds as Uncle Joe does, "I bet you thinking about that money you getting."

Sarah says, "Joe, shut up."

Dean just sits there with no response knowing this subject would arrive sooner or later. Johnny asks, "So how much money do you make?"

Rachel interjects, "That's none of your business. Dean, you don't have answer that."

Matthew asks, "Are you friends with the Duke and Duchess yet?"

"No. I haven't had time to sit and have tea yet. I basically just live there because it's a nice place to live. I'm not trying to make friends with any of the royal family. However, if it should happen I will let you know."

Joe, purposely trying to start a scene asks, "So what caused you to write the book?"

Being that everyone already knows the answer to the question it causes and uncomfortable silence. Everyone just sits quietly waiting to see how Dean responds. Dean, wishing he could disappear from the room just thinks of the best way to answer the question. He says,"Life, simple life caused me to write the book."

Joe continues, "Whose life?"

Sarah says, "Joe, that's enough."

"I'm just asking Manny…excuse me, I'm sorry, Dean, a simple question. So, Dean, whose life inspired you to write this bestseller?"

Dean just sits quietly. He is now wishing he never came to the house, knocked on the door and entered. He is trying to, without starting a family brawl, answer Uncle Joe's question. As he begins to answer tears are seen rolling down his face. He takes a deep breath and speaks. "I'm sorry."

Joe responds, "Sorry for what? I asked you a question. I didn't ask for an apology."

Matthew says, "Joe, that's enough."

Dean responds trying to end this conversation.

"I already know how you all feel. It's the real reason why I left and never returned. But, I've been doing some thinking and I know I owe everyone I know here in New Mexico an apology. I'm doing that, I am trying to do that. But there is nothing more I can give you except an apology. You just have to accept that."

Joe continues, "You can give some money or at least some credit, being that we helped you write the damn book. I mean talking about airing out your dirty laundry?"

Dean says, "I considered it as cleaning the dirty laundry."

Johnny responds, "More like making mad dough selling your dirty laundry."

Rachel continues, “It was kind of disappointing to see all our stuff just sitting there in black and white. You could have at least warned us.”

Heather now says,“You should have asked us.”

Joe responds, “He didn’t ask because he knew we would say no. Spending all that time in that damn London; he wasn’t living there, he was hiding out there.”

Sarah interrupts, "Okay, look damn it. Yes, Manny did a horrible thing. We all know it and we all are angry and disappointed of what he did, but the past is the past. He cannot take it back. He has apologized, just accept it and move on. Do you know how many people have done wrong and never apologized? He has at least apologized, just get over it and move on."

Joe's not finished. "I can't get over how he just threw our shit in a book and made millions of dollars and didn't even share the wealth. Not as much as a credit or thank you or even a mention of names."

Dean responds, "I didn't think you wanted the whole world to know that you were one of those dysfunctional stories."

Robert responds, "But according to your book there's nothing wrong with being associated with a dysfunctional family."

Dean responds, "If you wanted me to you could have simply asked."

Olivia chimes in, "Oh, as if you wanted us contacting you. You made it very clear before you left how much you hate this family."

Nicole adds, "And in the book too."

Dean answers, "I never hated any of you, I just hated that you hated me."

Matthew adds, "No one hated you, Manny."

"Well, you never showed me any love and you never accepted me."

Aaron enters the debate. "How could you say that? Every time you came over we always included you in everything."

"That's because your parents made you. As a child I always wondered what was wrong with me. What my mother did was not my fault. And every day you treated me as though it was."

Kendra angrily interrupts, saying, "I read that story in tears, because I could not believe that you thought the love I had for you was fake. I never mistreated you or did anything to make you feel unwanted."

Dean responds, "I never felt **completely unwanted.** Kendra, I know you loved me. I know you all loved me. I told you the book was fabricated. The more drama the more interesting, the more copies it sold. I am sorry, okay? I was desperate and this was the only thing I could think of to make something of myself."

Joe responds, "Oh, by throwing your family under a bus."

Kimberley interrupts, "That's enough. I'm not going to let you just kill my son over the dinner table."

Olivia speaks. "Yeah, well according to your son my mother is dead because of him. What the fuck was that? Why would you take credit for that? The letter never mentioned you."

"In so many words it did. And it is no secret why she didn't want to live anymore. I am not stupid, I know I was supposed to be aborted and if I was I am sure all of you along with your mother would be here pretending nothing ever happened."

Kendra blurts, "You had no right putting our mother in your book. That is our mother and you had no right just putting her in writing like she's some Lifetime character."

"I said, I'm sorry. What more do you want from me."

Johnny responds, "The book is public; how about a public apology?"

Joe says, "You see what you did, Mark? Having sex outside your marriage did nothing but create a monster."

Mark finally enters the conversation. "Okay, damn it, Joe, that's enough. You went way past the limit."

"No, your son went past the limit when he wrote that damn book. He ruined the family."

Dean finally loses it. "This damn family was already ruined before I ever got here. All the damn sexual, physical, and drug abuse in this family. I am not responsible for the shit that happened in this family, I just wrote about it. YES, I was wrong, I admit that, but I am not the one who created the dirty laundry. So, don't be mad at me."

Joe continues, "What you did was wrong."

"What do you want me to do, I can't take it back! You know what. I could leave. I am pretty sure you would all be happy if I just leave."

Dean stands, and as he does Sarah speaks. "Sit down."

"Aunt Sarah, thank you, but I have to go."

Sarah slams her hand on the table, which alarms everyone. "I said sit down. Now, look I don't care about the rest of you, but, I miss my nephew. Now, we are going to forget the past and enjoy a damn fucked up dys-fuck-tional family dinner. Now, Emanuel is staying, if you don't like it, then you can leave."

No one moves, Dean sits, and the room lapses quiet. After some time, Sarah breaks the silence. "So, Manny, how is it living in London? Is it nice?"

"Yeah, I like it."

Johnny responds sarcastically, "Is the grass really greener?"

Sarah responds to Johnny, "Okay, look, no more rude, sarcastic, angry remarks. If you don't have anything nice to say, then shut the hell up."

The silence reenters, but not for long. Sarah asks, "So, how big is Ben?"

Dean quietly laughs. "It's pretty big."

"Does it chime or make noise?"

Dean, ready to leave, responds, "I don't know."

"How can you not know? You live there don't you?"

"Aunt Sarah, I appreciate everything you're doing and have done, but I am ready to leave."

"You're not leaving."

Joe says, "Let him leave. Just like before."

Sarah is adamant. "Joe, shut up."

Joe responds to Sarah and Sarah comes back at him. Soon the whole table has chimed in to express their three year-long suppressed feelings. Dean just sits there in silence listening to the familiar sounds of his family arguing over the same issues. He finally sees the chance to leave. He stands and walks away. His mother notices and follows him. Kimberley says, "Where are you going?"

Dean hugs his mother then releases her.

"Mother, I love you and even this dysfunctional family, but it is clear that they cannot forgive me. I have forgiven them and apologized. I've done my part. I'm not going to waste my time on them. If they want to stay angry then let them, but I will not stay around them if they just want to be angry with me."

"You have to stop running away."

"I'm not running away this time. I apologized. I'm done."

Dean goes to exit the door, Kimberley grabs him. She looks him in the eye. "Could you at least write me; at least once a month? I'm your mother."

"Yeah, Mom. I'll write."

Kimberley grabs him and embraces him with a hug knowing she may never see him again.

"I love you, Manny."

"I love you too, Mom."

Dean leaves the doorway. Kimberley shuts the door and returns to the table that never stopped arguing. Kimberley interjects, "Hey, hey, hey! Ya'll can shut up now. He left."

Joe says, "That boy done ran away again."

Mark responds, “Shut up, Joe.”

Day 180 in New Mexico

Six months have finally come to an end. Dean Kyle Brent is packing his bags and heading back to London. His book signing tour is now over and it is time for him to return to the city that gave him his start as a successful writer. He has plans of writing his second book when he returns. A book about red ponies and purple squirrels to make sure no one sues him for stealing their life story. However, he knows he must do some things before leaving. Dean…Manny decides to make a visit and a couple of meetings before returning home to the city of London.

Dean arrives at his parents' house once again. This time without hesitation he knocks on the door. Mark answers the door. They embrace and Mark invites Dean in the house. Mark says, "I thought you left for London."

"I couldn't leave without saying goodbye."

"You left abruptly at the dinner."

"I just could not sit there and listen to that arguing. It's gotten old."

"Are you still upset with me, Manny? You don't still hate me do you?"

"Not anymore."

They both laugh.

"Son, I am truly sorry. I could have made much better decisions regarding my family. I never intended on making you feel the way you did. I wish you would have spoken to me."

"There was nothing you could do. What was done was done."

"I'm sorry about always arguing around you. Those things you heard, you should have never heard them. And…I'm sorry about the abortion…thing. I was just…I didn't want my wife to know what I did."

"Dad, I know."

"It is not your fault. She did not have to kill herself."

"I know that. I had plenty of time of thinking in London. That's why I came back. I had to make things right."

"So, do you plan on returning any time soon?"

"My book publisher is pushing me to write another book. I'll return for a book signing tour and this house will be my first stop."

"And what will this book be about?"

"Something completely fiction, like…orange bunnies and pink chipmunks; anything that won't get me in trouble."

They both laugh. Dean asks, "Is mother here?"

"No, she's not."

"That's okay. I already said goodbye to her. I just had to make sure I said goodbye to you before I left. I love you, Dad."

"I love you more."

They laugh, they share a hug and then Dean turns to leave. Before he does, Mark stops him. "Mom told me you promised her you would write her."

"Yeah, I did. I will."

"Don't forget me."

"I won't. Every letter I write Mom, I'll make sure to write you one too. I love you, Dad."

"I love you more."

"You always have to get the last word, don't you?"

"That's right, son."

Dean leaves the house and looks at the clock in the car and drives to a local restaurant. He parks the car and goes in. He walks towards a woman and smiles. She is looking out the window in expectation for someone. Dean calls out, "Hi, Aunt Sarah."

"There you are. I've been looking and waiting for you."

They embrace with a long time no see hug.

Sarah says, "So how are you? Is everything okay?"

"Yeah, all is well."

"So, what's up with this meeting? Do you need something?"

"No. I just wanted to apologize for everything. I knew the minute I entered that contest I was wrong. I was just so desperate."

"I've already forgiven you."

"Thank you. I also wanted to thank you for being one of the very few family members who loved me despite of the situation."

"Your family loves you. They have a strange way of showing it, but they love you."

"I know. But it's more than just saying it. You always showed it. I just want to thank you for that. You taught me how to give real love and I thank you for that."

"So how much longer are you staying in the U.S.?"

"I'm leaving today. I wanted to say goodbye to you. I didn't want to leave again like last time. You don't deserve that."

"Well, I thank you. You plan on seeing the rest of the family before you leave?"

"I don't have time. Besides, they'll just make me feel guilty. Everyone makes mistakes. The choices you have are to be bitter over them or to forgive. I choose to forgive, but until they do there's no reason to see them."

"Well, I thank you for thinking of me."

"I love you, Aunt Sarah."

"I love you more."

He smiles as he stands and they hug. With one last eye contact he heads to his car. Once again he gets in and checks the time. He drives to one more spot, another restaurant. As he gets out of the car he sees Kendra. He walks towards her and she turns towards him. They embrace.

"Kendra, I need you to forgive me."

"Manny, I love you. I will always love you. But I'm a bit angry and it is going to take some time for me to completely get over this, but that doesn't mean I haven't forgiven you."

"So, you forgive me?"

"Yes, Manny, I forgive you."

Dean embraces her once again. After they release, Dean speaks. "I just wanted to make sure I said goodbye to you before I left. I never completely felt a part of this family, but I will admit you did do your best to keep me included with everything. I thank you for that."

"No problem. Do you plan on returning or is this it?"

"I plan on writing my sophomore book. That should get me back here."

"You better be careful of what you write about."

"Yellow elephants and blue tigers is what I'm writing about."

They both laugh, and Kendra adds, "That should be an interesting book."

"Yeah, and it'll keep me out of trouble."

"I'm going to miss you."

"I'm going to miss you too. I promise to write this time."

"Thank you. Keep yourself out of trouble."

"I'll try."

"I love you, Manny."

"I love you more."

They both laugh. Kendra says, "Hey, that's Daddy's line."

They look at each other and smile. Kendra says, "You better write me."

"I will. I will."

They hug one more time and then part. Dean gets into his car and drives off to the airport.

At the terminal he goes through the regular harassment of security thanks to the current stressful times. As he walks towards his gate his agent sees him and runs towards him.

"Man, where the hell were you? We almost missed the flight. We got like five seconds to get on."

His agent and Dean run to make sure they don't end up spending the night at the airport.

As the flight takes off Dean looks down leaving his past behind once again. As he begins this ride from New Mexico to England he takes out his netbook and begins to type. His agent looks and asks, "What are you doing?"

Dean is smiling. "I'm writing a book about colorful animals."

Dean is standing in front of a podium brimming with microphones from many different television channels. In front of him are men and women from numerous radio shows, television shows, magazines, newspapers, and websites. He stands before them and speaks.

"Greetings everyone. I want to thank you all for coming today; I know you all could be elsewhere. I wanted to make a public announcement and hope that not only are all my fans watching here in this great country, England, but also my family and friends in America. As many of you may know, four years ago I wrote a book entitled, 'Essays from Dysfunctional Families.' Some of you may also remember a friend of mine Franklin Thompson sued me for plagiarism. The question everyone had was, did I write this book? The **answer is** yes. In our lives people enter and exit whether it is family, friends, classmates, co-workers or anyone else. During fellowship with people you have the chance to witness their life whether you take part or spectate. In my life I have come to realize the many stories that have unfolded in front of me were interesting and should be shared. However, being that they were not mine to share; for me to take them, and fabricate them in a book without the permission or consolation of the people who lived these interesting stories; I have come to publicly apologize to all of the lives who were hurt, offended, or made angry in any way. I am sorry to all those who felt my actions in writing this book were wrongful and deceitful. My intentions were simply to see if I had talent for writing the way my teachers said. In writing this book I had no intentions of hurting anyone in anyway and come forth apologetic hoping you can find it in your heart to forgive me and my actions. Again I apologize to every family member, friend, classmate, and/or coworker for exploiting their life and life stories without consultation or permission. Other than apologizing there is nothing more I can do to express how sorry I am and hope we can put this behind us. However, I am willing to republish the book with proper credits. If you are aware that your story is personally in this book let me know and I will add you in the credits and you will be given a percentage of the royalties. Just simply contact the publishers and give your name and address. Again I apologize for my action and hope you can forgive me. I love you and miss you all."

As he finishes the press goes wild. A man asks, "What was the purpose of the press meeting, other than apologizing?"

Dean responds, "When you come to the truth that you have done something wrong the best thing to do is to make it right. I am simply making my wrongs right."

Another loud ruckus is heard from the press. A woman's voice pushes through the commotion.

"In other news, is it true that you have finished your sophomore book? And if so when will it be released?"

"Yes, I did. It will be in stores next week."

Another voice: "Dean, what's the name of the book?"

"Pink Lions, Purple Tigers and Yellow Bears, Oh My: Stories From Colorful Animals. It's a children's book."

"Why the sudden change in book genre? And what took you so long to write your sophomore book?"

"Well, the only thing I knew I could do well is take a true story and turn it into a bestseller, but after being sued and the reaction from my family and friends back home I thought I could never write again. But after much thought I decided to write a creative book that is completely fiction and can't get me in trouble."

"Do you plan on returning home for a book signing tour like last year?"

"Yes, I do."

His agent walks towards the microphone and interrupts. "Sorry, guys, but that will be all for now. Dean will be making his TV and radio show tour starting next week. You can purchase his book at your nearest book seller next week. The book will be released on Tuesday. Thank you all once again for coming."

It has been seven years since the release of Dean's first book and three years since his sophomore book. He has returned home twice since the release of his second book. "Pink Lions, Purple Tigers and Yellow Bears, Oh My: Stories From Colorful Animals" has sold billions of copies just like his first book and became a bestseller and a love of children everywhere being translated in over twenty languages. Dean is now working on his first play, "Who Shot the Sheriff," which is a farce. The play will be produced at the Playhouse Theatre in the City of London.

Casey Bell, author of *The Diary of Stephanie Dane, 4Score*, and *Moving Forward* brings us *Literary Betrayal.* A story about a man who uses the life of his family and friends to write a bestseller. However, his family and friends are less then forgiving. follow Dean, the bestseller, and his family as they discover ways to get beyond the Literary Betrayal.

Emanuel Reed, Author

Casey Bell, author of *The Diary of Stehanie Dane, 4Score*, and *Moving Forward* brings us *Literery Betrayl.* Also playwrite of *CrazyFun.* Casey is a graduate of Kean University and a proud Uncle.

www.caseysamuelbell.com

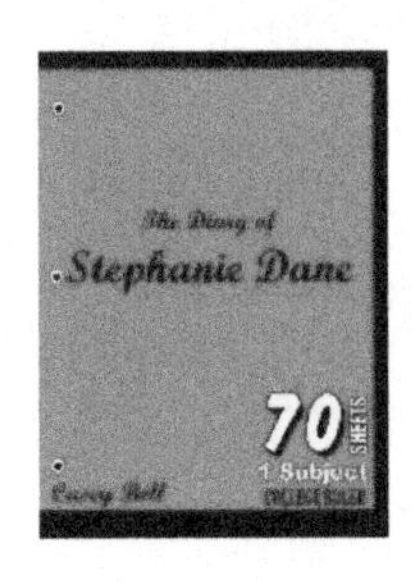

FOR MORE INFORMATION ON BOOKS BY CASEY

BELL VISIT HIS WEBSITES

http://authorcaseybell.weebly.com/

http://payhip.com/caseysbell

Thanks to my Editor: Michael Valentine
http://editor-ghostwriter.com/

bookcasepublishing.weebly.com

Made in the USA
Las Vegas, NV
14 January 2022